JOSHUA WORTHINGTON EAGLE
A STORY OF WORTH, TRANSFORMATION AND BALANCE

Sandi
Soar with the
Eagles!
Blessings
+joy
Samara

By

Samara C. Kezele Fritchman

In the publishing trade this book is called a 'hurt' book. The text is a pre-final edited version printed in error. So, please overlook the typos. **And enjoy the story.**

DEDICATION

This story is dedicated to two individuals
who stand out as wise owls along my life's journey.
First, Quale Pritchard, who, in 1978,
introduced me to God's love.
Second, John Replinger, who, in 1988,
adopted me as his granddaughter
and demonstrated God's love.

But those who hope in the Lord will renew their strength.
They will soar on the wings like eagles;
they will run and not grow weary, they will walk and not be faint.
—Isaiah 40:31

JOSHUA WORTHINGTON EAGLE
A STORY OF WORTH, TRANSFORMATION AND BALANCE

Publishing Information

Published by Samara C. Kezele Fritchman, Balancing Life™, www.balancinglife.com. First edition printed in association with Randall House Publications, PO Box 17306, Nashville, TN 37217

International Standard Book Number: (PB) 0-9672196-1-2
Library of Congress Cataloging Number: 99-094946
Printed in the U.S.A.
Adult Fiction

Cover Design by Sean Bonsell
    E-MAIL: infinite@clearlight.com
Editing by Val Dumond
    E-MAIL: jazzyval@aol.com
Illustrations by Kerry Weaver
    E-MAIL: kerry@redstone.net
Illustrations on page 7, 9, 11, 33 & 69 by Samara Fritchman
Reviewing someone's work is a silent servanthood, and those who do it are the unsung heroes and faithful friends. Thank you Marcie Fisher and Kerry Weaver for your special interest in my work. You were each giving of your time and ideas, which were greatly appreciated.

TABLE OF CONTENTS

Life is a journey, and hard work a reality,
but *balance* is the challenge
Resolve therefore to maintain a sense of balance
Avoid fanaticism and its illusions
Have a reality focus and seek greater purpose
Align who you are with how you feel, think and act
Be responsible, maintaining self-control
Care for your body, mind and spirit
Resolve to speak less and listen more
Communicate deliberately to inspire courage
Be a nourishing person
Live beyond anger
Be tender with the young, loving with the aged,
kind to the meek and tolerant of the unkind...
...and be all these things with YOURSELF

PREFACE

An eagle isn't meant to walk! Yet, Joshua Eagle walks with the chickens. How could an eagle be so misguided? The same way we are—by settling for mediocrity and familiarity! As a professional speaker, I'd often heard various versions of a tale about a sad little eagle that thought he was a chicken. The spoken story attempts to be motivational by encouraging listeners *not* to live their lives earthbound, when indeed, they were meant to soar. But, in these spoken versions of this motivational folktale, the eagle never figures it out. So, *Joshua Worthington Eagle* took flight—first in my mind and then on sheets of white paper. This 21st century fable depicts the rest of Joshua's story—the part never before told. He questions both mediocrity and familiarity, and his search for understanding leads him on a journey of discovery. Through struggle and confusion an eagle is reborn by the prophetic wisdom of Owl. Joshua's journey reflects poetically the human struggle for worth, transformation and balance—to alter misguided thinking and to see things differently.

My life had been a process that barred self-discovery. Always on guard, I practiced the art of reading others, until their feelings and needs were more obvious to me than my own. Never had I been free enough from the restraints of family, friends, or work to find the bottom line within myself. Who was I created to be? How could I live without having to justify my existence?

A major milestone in my life's journey started with the completion of *Joshua Worthington Eagle* in the fall of 1987. We often write to discover meaning. Through this story, I was not writing what I knew, rather I was writing to know and to learn. The story is about life—its joys, frustrations and confusions—as seen through the eyes of a misguided eagle. It was not until ten months after writing the story that I discovered its prophetic meaning. Life was not intended to be a single-sighted experience, nor was I intended to be too zealous about any one thing forfeiting a sense of balance. I needed to exercise my free will and become responsible for my choices. Joshua was a beginning for me.

May this book provide you with insight and inspiration—worth, transformation and balance.

6

CHAPTER ONE
J O S H U A ' S   B E G I N N I N G S

Gazing out beyond the majestic mountains toward the horizon of life, Joshua lingered in the moment. As he gazed upon another day, Joshua was anticipating moments to be lived. There is a joy, a balance, about his life that he cherishes now. Do not misunderstand what he means by *balance*. You never arrive at absolute balance, but you can always strive to achieve it.

Joshua sits and reflects with a peace and confidence that has become a part of him. "I am the eagle you have heard about, but now you will hear the rest of my story—the part they never tell. I must have been forgotten by the storytellers after my earlier years."

Joshua was born to soar in the heavens, yet in the beginning he thrashed about like a chicken, grubbing in the dirt. What a tragedy! Still, the world is full of those who settle for mediocrity. How easy it is to opt for a wrong way of life, thinking it is right because those around you are doing it. It is possible to live your entire life with a wrong perspective; Joshua Worthington Eagle was among the blessed.

CHAPTER TWO
L I F E   I N   T H E   B A R N Y A R D

Joshua's folktale began like this...

A farmer found an egg that had been laid by an eagle. Unable to return the egg to its own nest, he put it in the nest of a barnyard chicken. The hen sat on the egg, along with her own, and in time, the eaglet was hatched alongside the other chicks.

During his early life, the misguided eagle, thinking he was a rooster, did what chickens do. He scratched in the dirt for seeds and looked for insects to eat. He clucked and crowed the best he could, and he flew with a thrashing of his wings no more than a few feet off the ground. After all, that's what chickens were supposed to do.

THE MAGNIFICENT GOLDEN EAGLE HAS BEEN CALLED THE KING OF BIRDS. IT HAS BEEN USED BY GREAT EMPIRES AND NOBILITY TO SYMBOLIZE STRENGTH AND HONOR.

One day Joshua saw some magnificent birds far above him in the cloudless sky. With graceful majesty they floated on a powerful wind current, and soared with scarcely a beat of their strong golden wings.

"What beautiful birds!" said the eagle to the only family he knew. "What are they?"

"They are eagles—the King of birds," they said. "Not at all like us." Then they went about their day as always before, as chickens do. As the golden sun began to dim, lowering slowly behind the westerly mountains, Joshua and the other chickens nestled in for the coming night's darkness.

GOLDEN EAGLES ARE MORE POWERFUL THAN BALD EAGLES.
ADULT EAGLES HAVE FEW PREDATORS BESIDES MAN.

The next day began as all others. The sun rose, rooster crowed and activity began about the barnyard. Joshua jumped to the ground from his perch and started his daily routine of grubbing for insects in the dirt with the others.

"Good morning, Mother. How did you sleep?" inquired Joshua.

"Very well," replied his mother. "How about you?"

"I had a dream. I was flying high in the sky and looking down on the earth below. I felt as light as the air itself. I was strong and powerful, yet peaceful. It was so real! What did it mean?"

"Joshua, you shouldn't fantasize so much. Be content with what you have and who you are. It was only a dream," cautioned his mother.

"It was more than just a dream." Joshua replied. He stopped to recall his dream in detail before starting again, "I was flying toward a bright light. If I could have reached it, I would have been able to see things I have not been able to see before. However, as I flew I felt heavy and tired. Darkness fell upon me. Familiar feelings of confusion and fear returned. And this is how I feel, Mother. Fear engulfs me—fear of death, fear of rejection, fear of failure. Others surround me, yet the loneliness I feel is unbearable. I am lost among the familiar and I live with confusion. Am I crazy?"

SURVIVAL IN NORTH AMERICA HAS BECOME DIFFICULT DUE TO
HUNTING. GOLDEN EAGLES NOW BUILD THEIR NESTS PRIMARILY
IN THE ROCKY MOUNTAINS. THEY ARE ALSO FOUND IN
EUROPE, ASIA AND NORTH AFRICA.

"Oh, Joshua, it hurts to hear you struggle over such sad things," his mother offered comfort.

"But this dream was so real, as if someone is trying to tell me something. I just don't know what. And I question what this *what* could be. I feel like this dream is a reflection of my life. What does it mean?"

"Don't be so hard on yourself, Joshua. There are happy and unhappy animals of all breeds. That is life. Don't expect so much; it was only a dream," explained his mother, wanting to reassure him.

He thought for a moment about his mother's words. "Maybe it was only a dream, manifesting the worst in my mind. Life could be worse, that is true. But I feel like it should be better?"

This persistent thought lingered as he returned his attentions to grubbing for insects, pecking and scratching at the ground in search of his meal. He could not stop thinking about the dream, replaying it repeatedly in his mind all day long.

At nightfall, with an awkward thrashing of his wings, Joshua managed to perch himself on the corral fence board. He settled in comfortably and gave a good night glance at the other chickens as they headed toward the chicken coop. Although he was tired and wanted to sleep, he was fearful that sleep would bring more dreams full of questions and doubts. Then, just before dawn, he managed to drift off to sleep.

The sun glowed down upon the barnyard as another new day began. Joshua was slow to start his morning routine due to his sleepless night. He lowered himself from his perch to the ground. Once there, he began to think about something his mother had said yesterday.

"There are happy and unhappy animals of all breeds." Joshua began to wonder about the other barnyard animals. "Do others feel like I do or am I alone with these feelings? Maybe one of the other animals can explain the secret to life; maybe one of them will tell me."

GOLDEN EAGLES CAN WEIGH UP TO FIFTEEN POUNDS AND HAVE A WINGSPAN OF SEVEN FEET. THEIR BEAUTIFUL GOLDEN FEATHERS GO ALL THE WAY TO THEIR TOES.

Of all the animals he knew, he was sure the pig would feel as he did. "What a terrible life a pig has. It eats garbage; it cannot sweat; and, it lies around in mud! That's it, I will go talk with the pig," Joshua announced, and off he went in that direction. Arriving at the pig's pen, Joshua blurted out, "Are you happy, do you enjoy your life?" Pig looked at Joshua.

"Your life seems so grubby, dirty and isolated. It seems impossible for you to be happy," Joshua offered his righteous observation. He continued to look at the pig, who was covered with crusty mud. He felt comforted knowing someone else was as miserable as he was.

"In answer to your question, yes, I am happy. I know who I am and I do what I'm supposed to do. Is that not life in its fullest?" the pig replied.

Finding the response difficult to believe, Joshua was barely able to murmur a *thank you* while wondering how the pig could possibly be happy.

THE GOLDEN EAGLE IS MORE OF A SOLITARY BIRD THAN THE BALD EAGLE. GOLDEN EAGLES ARE GENERALLY FOUND IN REMOTE AREAS, AWAY FROM HUMAN SETTLEMENTS.

Deciding to look further for answers, he went to see the ranch horse. "Do you know who you are? Are you happy with what you do?" Joshua asked.

"What do you mean? Of course I know who I am. I am a horse. As for being happy with what I do, mostly I am. What is it that you need to know?" the horse questioned.

"I'm not happy, and I'm not sure why. Things don't feel right. I feel unbalanced and out of place in life. I'm wondering what it's going to take to feel right. I want to find answers to the nagging questions I have," Joshua uttered in one long, quick breath.

"As I said, I'm happy...for the most part," responded the horse. "I've never thought much about balance. There are times, though, when I feel a need to run free with no reins controlling my motion, making my own choices. Although, if I could change things, I'm not sure I would. I have come to know what to expect from my life here. Security, now that's important." The horse looked at Joshua as Joshua looked back at the horse. Then their attentions were drawn to the farmer who had entered the barn. The horse's owner was preparing for a trip to town in the wagon. The farmer pulled some brushes from the old wood trunk and began brushing the horse, who seemed to enjoy the soft strokes.

A YOUNG GOLDEN EAGLET RETAINS THEIR FIRST COAT OF JUVENILE FEATHERS FOR ONE YEAR BEFORE THEY MOLT AND GROW DARKER, MORE GOLDEN FEATHERS.

Joshua reflected on what the horse had said about security, realizing that it hadn't brought him any answers, only new questions. He found himself moving toward the rabbit's cage wondering what the rabbit thought about life. He was thinking about the security the rabbit had, protected by its cage.

He walked boldly up to the rabbit's cage, looked her right in the eyes and asked, "Would you change things if you could?"

"In a minute, if I could, but the lock to this cage is out there and I'm in here," replied Rabbit without the slightest hesitation.

"But you're safe in there. Isn't that important?" Joshua asked the rabbit. "You should be happy and you're not?"

"I'd rather be free to live with the risks. I have never known anything but this cage. Yet my heart and soul tell me it's not right. I long for something that just cannot be. How blessed you are, Joshua. If you long for something that is not, you are free to seek it. What are you seeking, Joshua?" The rabbit watched for his reaction.

Joshua realized he was *seeking*, but what? The dream had stirred something inside of him. He looked back at the rabbit and replied, "I don't know."

 GOLDEN EAGLES MAY NEST AT THE TOP OF TALL TREES; HOWEVER, MORE COMMONLY THEY BUILD A NEST ON THE EDGE OF A CLIFF OVERLOOKING THEIR HUNTING TERRITORY.

Joshua returned to his fence perch and reflected on what he'd heard. Pig's life seems so distasteful, yet he's happy. Horse, for the most part, is happy. It doesn't sound like she'd change things, even if given the choice, because she's found happiness in security. Then there is Rabbit, who's unhappy with security, wanting to change things, but can't, because it's beyond her reach.

Joshua, bewildered, confused and fatigued, settled down for the night. He couldn't make sense out of his friends' comments. Life must have more meaning to it, but for the life of him, he couldn't figure it out. Tired with his longing for understanding, he fell off to sleep hoping it would bring peaceful dreams.

Awakened by a fluttering of wings above, Joshua looked upwards toward the softly lit heavens. "Such beauty. What a beautiful sight. Such grace and freedom!" exclaimed Joshua. While watching the large, stately bird floating effortlessly through the sky, Joshua forgot his concerns.

He watched as a golden eagle guided itself toward a tall tree in the distance, possibly its home. As he watched, there were visions of movement in Joshua's mind that he didn't understand. For just a while longer, he focused his attention on the beautiful golden image.

A loud noise in the barnyard snapped him back to reality. He looked toward his home, at the other chickens, his mother, and beyond to the pig in its pen. The horse was hitched to a wagon preparing for another trip into town, and the rabbit lay motionless in her small cage. A deep depression fell upon Joshua, along with a strong need to get away from the barnyard, yet not understanding this need to escape.

"Why must life be so unfair—so disappointing—so pointless—so confusing—so many unanswered questions—why? I don't want to be a chicken, but what else can I be? My soul feels empty and my body feels tense. I can't seem to shake this anxious feeling. Where are these feelings coming from?"

CHAPTER THREE
THE NECESSARY JOURNEY

Joshua's thoughts stopped long enough for him to realize that he was no longer in the barnyard. He had, in fact, walked more than halfway to the distant tall tree. He was tired and the darkness of night was descending. He was more afraid at this moment than he'd ever been before, yet more excited. Where were these feelings of excitement coming from?

Drawn onward through the dark, Joshua silently moved toward the tree, as if compelled. He felt tired and frustrated, asking over and over in his mind, "Where's truth? Where's balance? Where's contentment?" It was a long walk to the eagle's tree, but Joshua kept on.

Physically drained, he fell to the ground at the base of its trunk, his mind exhausted to a point of numbness. Peering upwards through the dark, he again caught sight of the bird he had followed.

CHAPTER FOUR

O W L ' S   G I F T

"That's who you could be."

Joshua looked up, startled, "Who said that; where are you?"

"I did," said Owl who was sitting quietly on a low branch of the tree, only five feet from Joshua.

"What do you mean by that? You obviously do *not* know the truth. I'm a barnyard chicken, and my home is that nearby farm," Joshua insisted, as he gazed in Owl's direction.

"There is truth, if you seek it," Owl told Joshua.

"If there were truth, there would be a sense of balance in my life, I think," offered the confused Joshua.

"Oh, there is truth. Truth is objective; it's outside your own subjective perceptions. Truth is universal; it applies to you and to everyone. Truth is constant; it is as it was and as it will be. But what do you mean by *balance*?" asked Owl.

"I'm not sure. Things just don't seem right, but don't ask me what right is, because I don't know," he answered. "I want to know why I'm so unhappy? Why I don't have peace? Why I feel so confused? I talked with Pig, Horse and Rabbit about their lives, but they only cast more confusion on how I feel. And now you're telling me that this…" Joshua looked up, "…this majestic golden bird above me is who I can be!"

YOUNG EAGLETS PRACTICE FLIGHT FROM THEIR NESTS. WING MOVEMENT BUILDS MUSCLE, NOT COORDINATION. IT TAKES TIME TO LEARN TO CONTROL FLIGHT, ESPECIALLY LANDING.

Joshua continued to gaze at the golden eagle. Then he broke the silence. "This only causes more confusion. Why do you say that? Why do you want to confuse me?"

"If, as you profess to believe, that a barnyard chicken is all you can be, you wouldn't be here. A life was given to you. However, living your life is something you must do. It is something for which you must take responsibility.

"A life is not meant to be compared, one to another, as you did with the other barnyard animals. Pig is happy, but lives blinded to his ultimate demise. Horse has security in her slavery, but no freedom. Rabbit, though securely caged, has freedom in spirit. You cannot stand in judgment of someone's life when you're looking from the outside in. First, you have to look at yourself, from the inside. The answers you need will come from understanding the questions. Don't you see Joshua? You've been seeking answers to unknown questions. Seek first the clarity of your questions, then you will find your answers," said Owl.

"I don't understand what is happening. Who are you? Why are you telling me these things?" Joshua wailed.

"I understand your confusion; you are tired from the journey here. Now is not the time to sort these things out. Rest Joshua, we will talk again at daybreak."

The beautiful sunrise appeared to be brighter than Joshua had ever seen. He woke with a quiet feeling inside, although a bit surprised by his surroundings. He momentarily had forgotten his journey taken a few hours earlier.

As Joshua gained awareness, his thoughts turned upwards toward the top of the tree. The eagle was flying high above. Suddenly, Joshua remembered his conversation with Owl. Looking toward the near branch his eyes again met those of his mysterious friend.

"Good morning, Joshua. Did you sleep well?" asked Owl.

"Yes, quite well," Joshua replied as he fluffed out his feathers. "I remember your telling me I could be like that bird," he spoke as he looked upward at the eagle in flight.

"When you begin to look carefully, you will begin to see the questions for your life. If you can see the questions, you will find the answers," Owl replied. "Joshua, what's your heart, soul, mind and strength been asking?"

29

THE GOLDEN EAGLE IS ONE OF THE WORLD'S BEST HUNTERS. ITS HUNTING TERRITORY CAN COVER UP TO 160 SQUARE MILES. THEY PREFER OPEN LAND WITH SPARSE VEGETATION TO SEE THEIR PREY WHILE SOARING.

Joshua stopped and thought about that question. One word came to mind, *seeking*, but he didn't share it with Owl. After several thoughtful moments, Joshua focused on Owl and began to speak. "I'm not happy with who I am. What am I supposed to do with my life? How am I to live so that my life seems relevant? Does my even being alive matter? Would my disappearance leave a void?"

"Yes," Owl told Joshua, "but you must believe in yourself and take responsibility for who you are and all you can become."

"I don't want to be a chicken. I'm not even a good chicken. I have tried to do my best, but I hate grubbing for my food. I can't cackle well, and I've never felt comfortable roosting in the coop with the other chickens."

"You have been given so much more than you see. All these things that you see as inadequacies, I see as opportunities for you to learn the truth," said Owl. "The most difficult and confusing issues in life are often the very opportunities to gain knowledge and balance and to see life as it is. More importantly, to see things as they should be. Life is full of opportunities for growth. Look again, Joshua, at your home far in the distance. You can see it clearly, can't you?" Owl asked him.

"Yes," replied Joshua, "I can even see the animals in the barnyard, but what's the point? I've always had better eyesight than the other chickens."

"You do see well, but without vision. You accept your gifted sight as an error of life instead of the gift it is. Use what has been given to you. Exercise what you have—your heart, your soul, your mind and your strength," stated Owl. "You came to this tree on foot instead of soaring on the wings given to you. Don't you realize they were meant to be used?"

THE GOLDEN EAGLE'S SCIENTIFIC NAME IS AQUILA CHRYSAETOS.
AQUILA IS LATIN FOR EAGLE. CHRYSOS IS GREEK FOR GOLDEN.
AETOS IS GREEK FOR EAGLE.

"Use my wings to fly! When I use them, they hurt! And I know why, they are too large for a chicken's body."

"You do see well, but again without vision. Yes, your wings are large. But the aching is not from using them too much; rather, they ache because you don't use them enough. You were given what you need in life. Your wings are not too large; your understanding is too small. Your wings are not being used as they were meant to be. They are trying to tell you so," Owl stated.

"You talked with the other animals, but you learned nothing," Owl continued on. "You didn't seek knowledge, just idle conversation and justification for your own feelings. Listen to life with an open mind; seek knowledge and insights. They are limitless, so be open to learning. However, remember to always listen to the spirit deep within you for correct guidance. Your spirit is the essence of your existence. It's the very heart of who you are, the absolute foundation of your beliefs and it has been placed there by your Creator."

"I want knowledge and insights. I want to see with vision!" exclaimed Joshua.

"I believe you do," said Owl. "Your coming here is no coincidence. Therefore, I will share with you some information that can produce balance. If applied to your life it will enable you to live transformed from your current, limited self-perception. When I was younger and less wise, I was a *seeker* as you are now. I was given this information that I will now share with you. As you come to realize the value of these teachings, you will share them too."

CHAPTER FIVE
S E E I N G   C L E A R L Y   A N D
S E E K I N G   R E A L I T Y

Clarity is the first element...

Owl continued, "Clarity is the first element of balance. Sometimes we fail to know the needs of others, but more often we can see their needs more clearly than we can see our own. Many live their lives under an illusion that they will last forever. They waste their minds, their bodies and their spirit. They hope that the hand of fate will place them in a rich and wonderful place. This is not how life was intended to be lived.

"Joshua, do you understand your own mind, how it works and why?" questioned Owl.

"I don't think so," he replied. "I know it's full of thoughts and pictures and emotions, but as for how it works and why?—no, I don't know."

"When you take things in through your senses, your mind attaches emotions to the sights, sounds, smells, tastes or touches. All of these files are stored up inside your mind. They become your personal maps of this world; they cause you to behave in certain ways depending upon certain situations. And these ways become your habits.

"Your deeper mind cannot evaluate objectively. It can only mirror what you have given it to believe. As you grew up, you were bombarded with emotions and experiences. Your mind, through your senses, took it all in and you added your own meaning, developing your own patterns of acting and reacting. Your decisions are a result of your deeper mind the majority of the time. So Joshua, be careful of what you think about. Your dominant thoughts can become a self-fulfilling prophecy—the power of expectation is real."

Joshua looked away from Owl. In silence he thought about what Owl had shared. Was Joshua limiting himself with his current thinking by accepting his current situation instead of challenging it? Joshua, lost in thought, wondered about where his life could go.

What was Owl trying to tell him? Had he believed in falsehoods? If so, could he change his life? Could he become something more?

Joshua shifted positions, taking a moment to realize the sun had moved to a point directly above them. He again focused on Owl, ready to hear more.

"I can see you are seriously contemplating the things I say. You're wondering how you can change old habits, especially the ones that are not serving you honestly."

Joshua waited for Owl to continue.

"Look up and see the bigger picture. Use your potential for awareness and cherish your free will. Engage in new thought and action, acquire new ideas, cushion yourself from the negatives, and embrace the desire for change," stated Owl firmly.

Joshua listened carefully.

"Your heart seeks the Creator's desire for you. Now, you must become a conscious part of that *seeking*. The Creator knows your total capacity— your talents, your skills, your desires. The degree to which you use your potential will be your effectiveness and the directions toward which you lean will become your attitudes. Understand that your self-image is the accumulation of all the attitudes you perceive about yourself. It is the picture of yourself held in your heart and soul that controls your performance." Owl looked down at Joshua and nodded. "Joshua, how does your mind's eye see you—as a chicken or as an eagle?" asked Owl.

"A chicken is what I know. Is it truly possible to be an eagle?" Joshua asked, adding, "But how?"

"Many things have had an effect on your self-image. However, you have been misguided. Not out of malice or hatred, but worse, out of ignorance and mediocrity. Know this: you do not have to be a chicken, and the spirit within you, the one that brought you here, understands." Owl, still sitting on his branch, remained silent for a few moments giving Joshua time to think.

Stunned by the words ringing in his ears, Joshua thought of the love he had always received in the barnyard. Nevertheless, had he been misguided?

Owl looked down at Joshua. "Your perfection is to find out your own imperfection. See with Clarity. Focus on where you want to go, knowing where you are now, and remembering where you've been." Owl sat quietly before continuing to speak further on Clarity, starting with *purpose*. "Those who find contentment have clearly defined concepts for who they are. They have purpose. They look above the sun for answers while planning earthly directions, always remembering that adversity is an opportunity to further maturity and develop character. Doubts, fears and insecurities keep you from your potential. So be willing to trust. Far too many of us, Joshua, hinder our own lives. Quit belittling yourself. Self-respect is a necessity in order to keep on good terms with yourself. However, your ultimate worth is measured by your Creator's love for you, and Joshua, you are loved!"

"Have I hindered myself?" asked Joshua.

"You have, but don't let your past actions hinder you now. Learn from your errors and let those errors be the seeds for new growth," replied Owl. "You have great potential. Know that you have purpose, and have faith."

Noticing that the sun had moved from its position overhead, Joshua wondered if there would be enough time before sunset to hear everything Owl had to say about Clarity. As Owl continued to speak, Joshua turned his attentions back toward Owl in the tree.

"Other aspects of Clarity are *faith* and *wisdom*," Owl continued, as he readjusted his position on the branch. "Turn your faith to the promise of things hoped for and yet unseen. This is positive faith. There is no such thing as an absence of faith, but it can be consumed with its counterpart— fear. Belief in your fears, even those unseen, add no benefit to your life.

"Increase your ability to embrace change. We are changing all the time, yet most of us resist it. Excellence demands adaptability, flexibility, risk-taking, positive attitudes, a willingness to make mistakes, and above all—faith. Yes, have faith, especially in the face of change!

"We are given the freedom to choose whether we will go on or quit. Change requires a turning away from what feels secure, and because of this change is often avoided. To face change, you must believe that it will be for the best in the long run. Joshua, can you turn your back on what is secure?" questioned Owl. Although he wanted to say *yes*, he said nothing. Joshua sat motionless, thinking about how fears had crippled him in the past. Dare he now hope that change is possible?

Owl continued, "Wisdom is the combination of honesty and knowledge applied through experience. Wisdom is to say *no* and have the firmness of character to do so, saying no to those things that stand in the way of your growth. What good is a wise decision, if you give in to the easy way of doing things?

"Seek wisdom as you would seek air if you were flying too high. Do not let worry or procrastination destroy you. The effort you have to give is in releasing the situation and concentrating on something beautifully simple and uncomplicated, because many answers are just this simple," Owl said with conviction.

"I've been creating my own difficulties, haven't I? I have lacked clarity of thought. Back in the barnyard, I tried to find understanding through the eyes of the other animals. I lacked faith in my own intuitions. I needed to ask for wisdom; I needed to seek truth," Joshua responded insightfully as he looked at Owl awaiting a reaction.

Owl remained quiet, looking at Joshua with a smile in his eyes. Joshua could see Owl's pleasure in what he had already discovered.

Joshua bedded down for the night, yet his mind wouldn't slow. It was full of thoughts about Clarity and how he viewed himself and his future. From what Owl had shared, he knew that Clarity was the first element for a more balanced life.

"What is the next element?" Joshua asked Owl, who now seemed deep in thought.

"Congruency," Owl replied in a manner denoting that he was done speaking.

"Congruency, what does Owl mean by that?" Joshua wondered. "Tomorrow I will learn what Congruency is."

He returned his thoughts to Clarity, which had to do with seeing reality clearly. It had to do with who he was and what he could become. Reality became a focus, Joshua wanted to see things as they really were.

It was well into the night before he fell off to sleep—a deep sleep.

Awakening to a bright, shining sun, Joshua felt full of life, renewed in hope for his future. "Good morning, Owl." No response. He called out, "Owl! Owl?"

Owl was not on his branch and nowhere to be seen. A flood of fear and anger welled up in Joshua. "How could he have left me?" Then Joshua realized that he was reacting without conscious thought. He stopped for a moment and thought about what he now knew.

"I will have faith in those things unseen and use this time productively. What good does it do to know about Clarity if I don't use what I know," he spoke calmly to himself.

Joshua moved away from the tree and practiced his wing movements—those of an eagle, not a chicken. He carefully watched the majestic, golden bird above him in the sky and mimicked its movements. Working hard, Joshua was gaining strength. Soon he was able to lift himself slightly off the ground, awkwardly flying a few feet above it. Yet, not for any great distance, because his wings tired quickly.

"You're looking good," he heard Owl say.

Turning his gaze toward the tree, Joshua saw Owl perched on his branch. Joshua returned, appearing more like an eagle than a chicken.

CHAPTER SIX

I N W A R D   A N D   O U T W A R D   H A R M O N Y

We will continue today with the second element of balance—Congruency…

"Good morning, Joshua. You have used your time well. Clarity has built a new foundation for your life. Today we will continue with the second element of balance—Congruency," Owl told him. "This has to do with you, or more precisely, your feelings, your thoughts, your behavior and your attitudes. Congruency means to align yourself harmoniously. In order to be at peace with others you must first be at peace within yourself."

As Joshua opened his heart to what he was hearing, Owl continued to speak, "You grew up afraid of feelings because you heard things like… 'You shouldn't feel that way,' or… 'That's stupid to feel like that.' Of course, giving in to all your feelings wouldn't be beneficial. Such a surrendering would lead to jealousies, lies, concealment and even death.

"Feelings can be negative or positive or both for any given situation. You don't pick and choose your emotions toward a given situation; they just happen—automatically. But too often, you deny your negative feelings because they are negative and in doing so, you make them worse. Negative feelings are like a fever; left untreated they can burn to the core of your existence and ignite your heart with anger. Accept them, admit them, face them. Only then will you be free from their hold. Face the negative emotions in your life. See them for what they are—a signal that you're out of balance. Emotions such as grief, anger and hurt ultimately turn on you if not recognized and dealt with," Owl completed.

Owl looked at Joshua to see if he had understood. He had, so Owl continued to speak, turning his focus to the importance of thought. "Thought involves knowledge and taking the time to apply it. Never forget that negative thoughts feed on fear and starve on faith. As you think, you move through life. You are here today because your thoughts brought you, and you will be in the future where your thoughts lead you. During your lifetime, you will see the results of your dominant thoughts."

"I know what you're saying!" exclaimed Joshua. "I have the ability to rise above my feelings by choosing my thoughts. And, I should think about pleasant things, deliberately turning my thoughts to something good and wise."

"You do understand," Owl confirmed to Joshua as he continued to speak, changing his focus again.

"Behavior involves going the right length and no further. No behavior takes place in isolation; it will always affect others. Nor can any one act of behavior be traced to a single cause. Always, it seems that you know without being told when you have acted unkindly or behaved unjustly toward someone.

"Feel your feelings when they occur, then choose your thoughts. And never give yourself the right to abandon your obligation to manage your behavior. If the past has taught you anything, it is that every cause brings its effect—every action has a consequence. Behavior is a personal responsibility."

Without hesitation Owl continued, "Attitudes are a reflection of who you are. Your attitudes toward life determine life's attitudes toward you. Before you can achieve a positive and productive life, you must form positive and productive attitudes. Your attitudes are formed from the actions you choose based on your feelings or your thoughts. There are two choices in life: accept conditions as they exist or accept your responsibility for the ability to change them or view them differently."

Joshua looked above and saw the sun moving quickly in the direction of the western mountain range. Reflecting, he said, "I'm surprised at how fast the day went. I do understand. I can take spontaneous negative feelings resulting from a situation and turn them into positive thoughts, followed by productive behavior, resulting in quality attitudes." He looked at Owl and said, "It's important that I work these aspects of myself together harmoniously, isn't it?"

"With harmony, yes," said Owl, "and that is congruency. Whenever a situation occurs, at any given moment, the immediate response will be a feeling. Unfortunately, too many of us condemn ourselves for negative feelings. We shouldn't, because we'll never arrive at a point where only positive feelings exist. The problem with negative feelings is acting upon them without thinking things carefully through. Thought is the opportunity for serious consideration, for reasoning things out, and for the ability to visualize and develop an intention or plan. It is your ability to ask for prayerful guidance.

"Thought is your intellectual ability. When you take the time to think before you act, your behavior is more likely to be appropriate and productive. As a result of this you will form quality attitudes toward yourself, others and life." Looking at Joshua, Owl asked, "Can you see how your feelings are the *state of your soul*; how your thoughts are the *state of your will*; how your behavior is the *state of your strength*; and, how your attitudes are the *state of your spirit*." Owl's tone of voice denoted the importance of what he had just said and Joshua felt no need to answer.

Taking a cleansing breath, Owl continued, "Congruency also has to do with your values. Your values are a basis for your life and help establish your morality. Morality is concerned with the acts of choice, and choosing the right direction leads to peace and balance. Practical common sense is prudence. Going the right length and no further is temperance. Honesty (give and take, and keeping promises) is justice. Courage in the face of change is fortitude," Owl concluded.

By the end of the second day, Joshua knew about the first two elements of balance. He was looking forward to learning more and wanted to ask Owl about the next element. But, Joshua sensed that Owl had said all he was going to say for the day.

Joshua reflected, "Clarity enables me to see myself and my life more realistically, gaining more wisdom and a sense of purpose. Congruency helps me to understand myself. I'm able to see how I can change my attitudes by paying closer attention to my feelings, thoughts and behavior. How interesting—my feelings, thoughts and behavior determine my attitudes; my attitudes help determine my feelings, thoughts and behaviors." That night, before falling to sleep, Joshua gave thanks for being at this tree.

Joshua rose early the next morning, needing to be alone for awhile. He wished—no, he hoped—about a new beginning for his life. He had been out practicing his flying and was looking more and more like the bird he now knew he could be. The majestic bird, which he had followed to this tree, flew high above his head and Joshua knew he would be flying high in the heavens soon.

"Maybe I know enough now," thought Joshua. With that Joshua turned his sights upward and with a strong pumping motion of his wings, he began to climb into the sky.

Higher and higher he flew, full of himself and ideas of returning to the barnyard to show them who he really was. His mind was so busy thinking, he didn't notice how tired and heavy his wings had become until he realized he could barely move them. In a flash, the reality hit him—he was far above the ground and falling quickly.

Joshua wanted time to stop, or at least turn back to a time when his feet were on the ground. He was totally out-of-control.

As he was falling earthward, he thought feverishly, "Why was I so smug—thinking I knew it all, feeling invincible, and wanting to show off to my friends?" Joshua realized now how selfish and prideful he was capable of being.

As the ground grew nearer, Joshua spread his wings full out with the last bit of strength left in him. "It's working, I'm gliding, still too fast, but it's better than falling."

With that thought he hit the ground hard and tumbled beak-over-tail until he came resting to a stop, only a few feet from the tree.

There he lay.

"Too often we rush headlong into something that seems to be instant happiness (because we want what we want when we want it), all the time telling ourselves we can right any wrongs later," spoke Owl quietly. "If you had died from your pride and arrogance, how could you have righted that?"

"I thought I knew enough and I wanted the others to see how much I'd learned," Joshua told him with remorse.

"As of today you need to accept more responsibility and control for what you think and do. Last night I could tell that you were curious about the next element. Like so many before your time, you thought you knew it all just because you understood Clarity and Congruency. You became full of yourself, then selfish. But, these are only part of what you need to understand if you truly want to achieve a greater sense of balance." Owl paused for a moment to collect his thoughts, while Joshua tried to regain his composure from his nearly fatal fall.

"The experiences you have in life are there for you to learn from. Your most recent experience shows you how little you know about self-discipline and the importance of controlling your actions. You acted on impulse and almost killed yourself. Reflect on what you have learned from the first two elements, but realize you have not seen the complete picture. Clarity and Congruency are building blocks in the Hierarchy of Balance. This knowledge, that you now have, should be combined with knowledge you have yet to gain."

Joshua ached as he sat on the ground listening to Owl. The pain was a reminder that he did have more to learn.

CHAPTER SEVEN
G O V E R N A N C E   A N D
R E S T R A I N T

Control is the third element of balance...

"Control is the third element of balance," stated Owl in a louder, more direct voice. Joshua knew his tone was directed at his recent actions.

"You won't always be able to control what goes on in the world around you, but you can always control your actions and attitudes toward it." Owl continued, "What is a crisis? It is not what's out there. It is your attitude about the situation. If you don't know what to do about a situation, wait awhile, an answer may come. You must recognize past hardships for what they are; they are parts of your personality. But you must not let past events become crutches to lean upon whenever you think you need an excuse. You must learn to exercise control over your behavior."

"I didn't exercise much control over myself this morning," replied Joshua. "I let my feelings and my thoughts carry me away, almost to the point of my own destruction." Joshua could barely stand to hear his own words.

"You are learning, and you will continue to learn all the days of your life. When you have learned to control yourself, you will be of great use to your Creator," Owl responded.

"Control is a power, that is, a *bridled*-power. Keep a tight rein on the issue of power so you'll have the ability to love with softness and act with strength. Power comes from a sense of self-confidence. However, without Control you will lose that very confidence. The essence of power is the ability to handle the demands of life.

"Unfortunately, power is often misused. What are the reasons behind a need to control others by being clever? Is it to feel more in control? Why can't everyone just live honestly and openly, without ever scheming and trying to appear something they are not? Those who control others will ultimately find themselves out-of-control."

There was a pause. Then a silence filled the air. Joshua looked up toward the place where Owl sat, only to realize he was gone.

"Where did he go?" wondered Joshua, feeling alone. Too tired and sore to think beyond that one question, Joshua fell asleep, giving his injured body a chance to mend. Somehow, Joshua knew Owl would be back with the first light of dawn.

Owl had needed to spend time with himself in thought and prayer. Then he returned to his home. After leaving Joshua at the base of the eagle's tree, Owl had flown in the direction of the nearby mountains. He landed on a tall fir tree at the base of a high peak. Looking into the eyes of his beloved mate, Owl spoke softly, "It feels good to be home, if only for this one night. I will need to be there for Joshua tomorrow morning."

"Tell me about Joshua; who is he? Is he another precious soul placed in your path?" asked Owl's beloved.

"Yes, he is. Three evenings ago, I was quietly reflecting as I was sitting on a branch of the eagle's tree. Joshua, a misguided golden eagle, walked up to the tree in the darkness of the night. His thinking has been misguided from birth; he thinks he's a barnyard chicken. Yet, his spirit, which cries out for answers to unknown questions, pushes him onward. So I was placed at the tall tree to share with Joshua the knowledge of *balance*, to help him clarify his questions so he can find his answers."

"How is he doing?" Owl's loving mate asked. She moved close to him, feeling the warmth of his feathers and the love that he had for her in his heart. Owl had the same feeling, and before he answered her question, they both sat still, enjoying their bond. Then Owl broke the silence by saying, "He is a willing learner."

Their conversation turned from Joshua to each other, as they enjoyed the short time they had together before Owl would return to the eagle's tree.

CHAPTER EIGHT
P R E P A R E D N E S S
A N D   S T A T E

Today I will talk about Condition…

Joshua woke up hearing a movement on the branch only a few feet from his head. "Owl, it's good to see you. I knew you'd be back!"

"How's your body doing, Joshua?" asked Owl, but he didn't wait for an answer. "You not only hurt your body in the fall, but also your mind and your spirit. You must recognize your existence is threefold: physical, mental and spiritual. I've shared with you the first three elements of balance. Today I will talk about Condition," Owl told Joshua.

"It is important to care for yourself and place an importance on your Condition. You need to have a sense of joy and seek humor in the course of your life and live relaxed by combining labor, learning, love and laughter. To grow in knowledge enables you to care for yourself. This way you will remain alert. Good health and a clear mind are essential for growth. What good does it do to know about Clarity, Congruency and Control unless you apply them to Condition and apply Condition to them?

"First you need to see things more clearly. Second, you must come to understand yourself better. Next, you must focus on discipline. Then you can choose to Condition yourself. Once you can see the importance of Condition, you can work at making yourself physically fit, mentally alert and spiritually sound."

Owl elaborated, "Condition in the physical sense is exercise. It is keeping fit so your body will have the endurance life requires. Condition in the mental sense is knowledge. It is keeping your mind fit by a continual focus on learning. There is no limit to the amount of knowledge your mind can hold. Condition in the spiritual sense is staying in touch with your Creator. It is nurturing the spirit within you through prayer and praise."

Joshua stood still, thinking about what he had heard. He spread his wings fuller than ever before and began moving them up and down. His mind felt open to knowledge, knowing that the spirit within was alive and willing.

Joshua walked away from the tree deliberately thinking on good things. He caught a glimpse of the golden bird—the one he was meant to be—and for the first time he felt, truly felt, this reality. As he walked, he circled back to the tree and realized what a habit it was to walk instead of fly. He would break this habit, day-by-day, as he continued to be transformed beyond his old existence.

Joshua spent the afternoon exercising his wings, and testing his abilities. There was an ache from the movements, but it was a good ache.

When he returned to the tree, Owl said nothing more as Joshua realized a greater sense of balance within. Joshua started to walk away from the tree again. Then he caught himself, now knowing that he was capable of flight. He looked upward and with a strong, downward movement of his large wings, he raised himself into the air.

By late evening, Joshua could gracefully soar above the ground using his large wings—and it felt right. However, he stayed close to the ground, partly because he was still sore from his fall, but mostly because he wanted to think and act more deliberately. After several low but graceful flights above the ground, Joshua returned to the tree.

Joshua and Owl spent most of the early evening separate. It was a quiet, reflective time for both of them. Then, before bedtime, he and Owl spoke quietly together, reflecting on all they had discussed and some about what they would be discussing, until it was time to sleep.

The sun's rays erased the darkness as a new day began. Joshua woke up and began to stretch out his wings. They were sore and stiff and he felt the intensity of the past four days. Joshua did miss his friends. He momentarily felt a longing for the barnyard and was frustrated by his aches and pains. He realized that he had hardly given much thought to the only home he'd known before now.

Joshua recalled the first four elements: Clarity, Congruency, Control and Condition. Before they went to sleep, Owl had shared the name of the fifth element of balance; it was Communication. Owl had explained how too many try to communicate without the knowledge of the first four elements. Owl had said, "How do you think you can communicate effectively if you don't see the realities of your situations, or have never stopped to understand how your attitudes affect what you say. In addition, to communicate without self-control often causes trouble. Further, it's important to have a sound body, mind and spirit so that you have the endurance, knowledge and love it takes to communicate, and to communicate in a way that helps build closer relationships." Those were the words Owl had concluded with last night, and the words that Joshua had thought about as he had fallen asleep.

"Good morning Joshua, how are you feeling today? Better? Oh, the stiffness will go, Joshua, and the pain will leave. Yet, your memory of being out-of-control hopefully will remain, as a healthy reminder," added Owl to his greeting.

Owl watched Joshua. He could see a change in Joshua that was reflected in his appearance. It was the beginning of his transformation. Owl rejoiced quietly and humbly, for he was watching a rebirth, a renewal of a one of God's creatures. He was filled with joy.

The day began to seem brighter to Joshua. His pain and stiffness were less than yesterday; he was mending. The anticipation of what he would learn today began to well up inside him. Joshua shifted his position on the ground, looked up at Owl, and waited.

CHAPTER NINE
TO IMPART AND CONVERSE

Communication is the fifth element of balance...

"Communication is a vital part of your existence and it is the fifth element of balance," Owl began. "Words are symbols and to be misunderstood is painful for anyone. You want to explain and explain until you get your message across. Sometimes you fail because you choose unwise words; sometimes it's because of an unwilling ear.

"You, just like everyone else, want to be understood. Unfortunately, and far too often, you receive criticism or defensiveness instead of understanding, because others have their own shortsightedness. When you desire a connection with someone often you receive withdrawal or anger or blaming or joking, all of which can be attempts to avoid intimacy. Or vice versa, you could be the one causing division.

"So listening should become your most important communication skill, Joshua. Strive to avoid listening in only a partial manner; instead, listen fully. A good listener enjoys many friendships. Everyone needs someone to talk with at great length on all subjects without regret."

Joshua thought about the truth of Owl's last statement. He thought about the times when he'd only listened halfheartedly, because he was too focused on himself. "Listening is a very giving gesture, isn't it?" Joshua asked, knowing it was. He also reflected on his past, knowing that he had fallen short of giving this gift of himself to others.

"More can be learned from listening than talking. However, when you choose to talk, ask questions to gain information and gently guide others toward their own answers. Communicate to build up, not to tear down.

"Communication can be likened to a tool box full of a variety of tools, each appropriate for different tasks. Communication should never be a tool used to control others for your own ego's sake; to tear down others in an effort to build up yourself; or, to win at the loss of others.

Your words can build or destroy. What you say can give courage or increase fears. Often, you never know when something you've said is used by someone to make an important decision," Owl explained.

Joshua thought back over several past conversations he'd had with his family and friends in the barnyard. The words he'd heard from others had helped him make decisions, some good and some bad. He also realized that his words, often spoken out of confusion, frustration and fear, must have affected his friends.

"I hope my past words haven't caused too much damage. What if I have harmed instead of helped?" Joshua inquired feeling quite concerned as he recalled past conversations.

"That is a chance we take whenever we open our beaks. Remember, it is everyone's responsibility, not just yours. Although, having the knowledge of Clarity, Congruency, Control and Condition gives you a stronger foundation for quality Communication," he said.

"Remember, Joshua, these elements of balance are not absolute and are not an obtainable goal of perfection. They are places to begin, starting points, areas to focus on for growth. You will never arrive at absolute balance. *Life is a journey, hard work a reality, but balance is the challenge.* Abundant life becomes possible when you understand where the pieces of life fit together. Joshua, it is important that you understand this and understand it now. Do you?" Owl questioned, waiting to hear the reply.

"I believe so," replied Joshua. "I should not aim for perfection because it's an ideal. These elements of balance are guidelines. I'll remember this, I promise," he said, trying to sound assuring.

Joshua had been with Owl for five days. It had been six days since he had seen the barnyard, his home—the only one he'd ever known. Joshua stretched out his wings and looked at himself, truly realizing his ability to be more. Did he have the fortitude to face the changes? This started Joshua wondering about his life. "How could I ignore what I've learned? Why would I want to?" Joshua stood still as he wondered what would be in store for his future. He wanted to ask Owl about the next element, but he decided not to. Tomorrow would be here soon enough. While he was thinking, Joshua faded out of consciousness, drifting into a world of dreams.

The next day was the brightest and warmest morning of them all. Joshua was stunned by the beauty and by the sounds and the smells of the world around him. He heard the wind rustling through the bushes and birds chattering to each other as they flew above him. There was a freshness in the air that smelled of spring. He had slept well, while giving in to the realization that his life would be the life of an eagle, a life above the ground. He sat there looking up at the clear blue, bright sky with all the sights and sounds of other birds briskly flying about in its vastness. He looked at the ground and realized that he would be leaving his earthbound life behind. For a moment that thought saddened him, but quickly it was replaced with thoughts of the sky and the wise owl. With that, Joshua looked at the branch and caught the eye of his teacher and friend.

"Good morning Joshua, it's a wonderful day for our last day together," said Owl.

Joshua wondered about Owl's last statement. Would he never see Owl again? Who would guide him, direct and teach him, or answer his questions?

CHAPTER TEN
R E L A T I O N S   A N D
C O N N E C T E D N E S S

We will speak about Closeness, the sixth element of balance...

"Today, we will speak about Closeness, the sixth element of balance. You are here on this earth to interact with others and that's not always easy to do. Your relationships with those around you have to do with Closeness. How can you ever have nourishing, healthy, stable relationships without understanding the importance of the first five elements? And understanding isn't enough, you must incorporate this knowledge into your daily life.

"Ideally, you enter into relationships to share. Of course, what you say and how you say it is largely responsible for the quality of your relationships. But before you can do this, you need to have vision, self-understanding and discipline, along with endurance. Each of these elements contribute to a greater sense of balance. Far too many try to find all the answers to their questions of loneliness and confusion from this element, the highest level. It cannot be done without the knowledge and exploration of the others.

"Many find excuses for themselves at this level. Often they believe that the problems in life are there because of the personalities, attitudes and inadequacies of others." Owl paused for a moment as Joshua thought about this last statement.

Just as he was about to speak, Owl continued, "When you have a problem with someone else, you're often the one who needs to change. Your encounters with others can be nourishing or they can be toxic. They can provide joy and well-being or they can deprive and frustrate. It's your responsibility to tell the difference between the two. You need to rely on your knowledge of balance to discern. The ability to be discriminating in your relationships is an on-going learning process. There are no ideal individuals. If you were all the things that you expected from others, the result would be perfection. You'd be perfect in forgiveness, faithful in love, and devoted to the welfare of those around you.

"You are not perfect; you need to watch out for jealousies, spite, anger, hate and revenge. These will tear, not only at your relationships, but also at your very existence. Jealousy makes you compare your lot with another and there can be no comparison, for no two are alike. Freedom to be who you are and to allow others the same builds faith and trust. You will never keep someone in emotional bondage without being in bondage yourself." With that Owl stopped speaking and sat quietly on the branch until he added, "And the closest relationship possible is with the One who made you."

Joshua sat quietly in his place on the ground. He looked about, again noticing the beauty of the day and the fullness of life. He looked up toward the top of the tree, the tree which had become his home. He saw other birds flying above. The one he'd originally followed was landing on one of the highest branches. There was a quality in that bird which had drawn Joshua away from his life in the barnyard. It was something that he had to know more about, something he had wanted to be.

"I'm so fortunate," he caught himself saying aloud.

"Why is that?" Owl asked.

"Oh, I was just thinking. I was thinking about how lucky I am to have found my way here."

"Luck, you say?"

"Well yes, I guess, what else?"

"Possibly a burning desire deep within you, or maybe it was your spirit within you yielding to your Creator's Spirit, or then again, it could have been *luck*, but I doubt it. It's not so much a need to analyze why you're here, but rather what are you going to do next?" Owl looked at Joshua.

Now that thought was simultaneously scary and exciting for Joshua.

"What have you learned?" Owl asked.

"Well, I know that there are elements, or aspects of life that I can focus on and build upon. These elements are like building blocks, yet they are interrelated.

"Because of *Clarity*, I'm seeking reality and wanting to see clearly who I am. Because of *Congruency*, I'm desiring to understand myself and become harmonious. Because of *Control*, I'm striving to act with discipline and governance. Because of *Condition,* I'm hoping to care for my body, soul and spirit maintaining a state of preparedness. Because of *Communication,* I'm learning to hear and impart information, feelings and ideas. Finally, because of *Closeness,* I'm understanding that I can love and be loved by developing a connectedness with others. I know these things, but can knowing truly make a difference?" Joshua tilted back and looked up at the familiar and friendly face of Owl, wondering how he would respond to what he had just said.

"What do you think?"

"I want to say *yes,* but yes will mean leaving behind all that I have been. That scares me!" answered Joshua.

"Joshua, you will not be leaving behind what you've been or have known, but rather you'll add to it what you've learned and become. If you want to transform with this new knowledge, you must go beyond where you are now. You will never be successful in life by just being a spectator— a gatherer of knowledge. You will never enter into the joys of a balanced life by simply being an admirer of life, sitting on the sidelines."

Nightfall was settling in, as their sixth day together was ending. They had been talking all day. Now in silence, time seemed irrelevant. Owl stretched his wings then lifted up into flight for some well-needed exercise. Joshua watched Owl as he flew, never taking his eyes off of him until Owl returned to the tree.

Owl broke the silence, "If balance is your desire, then focus on faith and diligence. Each is one side of a scale. They both need to be present. Faith is your belief and diligence is your action. It is not difficult to have a dream, but it often ceases at that point. The willingness to follow through, the determination to look impossibilities in the eye and trudge onward must be practiced. Tonight, Joshua, you will begin your transformation by accepting your new beliefs as reality. Continue to grow and take risks. Along life's road there will be those who will discourage you, very often out of ignorance, not realizing the possible affects of their words upon you. Grow to trust your Creator and then yourself. Opportunity has been known to pound on a door, yet go unnoticed. This chance we've had to share did not. Joshua, never stop growing. Aim high and don't go backwards. We will see each other again someday. Until that time we'll carry each other within us." With these last words, Owl spread his wings, lifted up off the branch and disappeared into the night's darkness.

CHAPTER ELEVEN
JOSHUA'S TRANSFORMATION

"Why did he leave? When will I see him again?" Joshua knew his time with Owl, at least for now, had ended.

Truly, it had been a splendid time. Joshua tried his best to be scared at the thought of being alone, but he just couldn't make himself frightened. He was an eagle, a majestic fowl, King of the sky and that was his future.

As he slept that night, Joshua dreamed about his six days with Owl. He could see in his mind's eye the bird he was meant to be. He dreamed of flying high in the sky, soaring gracefully on his large wings. There was a bright light that enabled him to see both familiar and new places. He felt as light as air, soaring effortlessly. The memories of his life were in his mind, his future was a vision. He knew his future would be exciting. If he was ever afraid his dreams wouldn't come true or that they might sound foolish, he wouldn't talk about them. He would work faithfully and diligently toward realizing them. All of this, he dreamed, until he awoke.

"What is this?" Joshua jumped up, startled by the sight around him. It took a few moments for him to realize where he was and what was on the ground around him. Feathers, many feathers, his feathers!

"What happened, what's wrong with me?" He looked at himself the best he could, cocking his head in every possible angle. "I seem to be all right, but what are all these feathers doing on the ground?"

THE BIBLE MENTIONS THE EAGLE IN SEVERAL SCRIPTURES. IT IS PRAISED
FOR ITS SPEED OF FLIGHT, POWER AND STRENGTH. THE EAGLE REFERENCES
IN THE BIBLE ARE BELIEVED TO BE ABOUT THE GOLDEN EAGLE SINCE IT'S
THE LARGEST EAGLE.

Joshua looked at the ground, at all the feathers—his feathers—and then, quickly he said aloud, "I'll ask Owl, he'll know." He turned his gaze toward Owl's branch only to remember his departure late the night before.

"That's right, what am I thinking? He's gone."

With a beat of his wings, Joshua moved from his nest of feathers on the ground to the closest branch in the tree.

"That was easy," he thought as he compared this light flight to his previous ones. He felt lighter and why not, with all those feathers on the ground, why wouldn't he?

Joshua sat on the branch and looked at the ground, recalling his dream.

"Was it a dream, or did it happen?" he wondered. It was after Owl had left; he was sure he'd fallen asleep. He had dreamed of flying—like eagles fly! He was high in the moonlit sky, soaring majestically on the wind's current. As he flew, the wind gently beat against his body and feathers loosened and some fell out, floating off into the night's air. He was flying out of the darkness of his previous life into light. His flight was effortless and his focus was on the future—his future.

"My future!" Joshua returned to reality. "Did I make that flight or was it in my mind?" Whichever, Joshua's reality was transformation. He had shed his earthbound existence for a skybound future. "There's no going back," he said. "With all I know now Owl, I can't settle for life as it was, can I? This dream, or flight, was so much like my dream a week ago. Had it been a vision?" Joshua knew Owl wasn't there, but it helped to talk to him anyway.

It was Joshua's seventh day at the tree, a place that seemed secure to him now. How interesting, since seven days ago the barnyard was secure—the tree was not.

"I wonder if this is how life is?" Joshua thought aloud. "As you move into each new area of your life, it eventually feels secure. I'm transforming, just as Owl had foretold." It was now impossible for Joshua to settle for life as it used to be.

With one beat of his golden wings, he was airborne. A few more beats of his powerful wings and he was high into the heavens gazing at the world below him. Far in the distance to the east was the barnyard and to the west the mountain range covered with glistening snow that reflected the early-morning sun. And, there, between the two was the tree, his current home.

DOES THE EAGLE SOAR AT YOUR COMMAND AND BUILD HIS NEST ON HIGH? HE DWELLS ON A CLIFF AND STAYS THERE AT NIGHT; A ROCKY CRAG IS HIS STRONGHOLD. FROM THERE HE SEEKS OUT HIS FOOD; HIS EYES DETECT IT FROM AFAR. JOB 39: 27-29 (NIV)

"What is out there beyond those mountains?" he asked. "Do they hold my future?" Just as he had been drawn to the tree, now he was feeling drawn to the mountains.

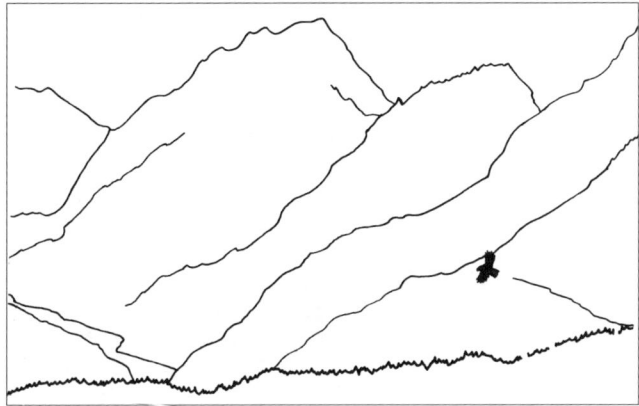

He was flying west when he suddenly shifted his wings into a proper position for a downward glide, circling slowly back toward the tree. As he approached, he saw the other birds flying about and he thought how he would get to know them—someday. However, today would be a day of rest. Tomorrow he would return to the barnyard and then, well, he would know what to do when the time came.

He had spent hours in the sky, yet the time had passed like minutes. Nightfall was moving in; the sun was setting behind the range of mountains that seemed to be calling. Bright oranges and reds filled the sky as peacefulness settled in upon him. Six days he had spent with Owl, learning something new each day. In addition, each day's lesson built upon the last and prepared him for the next. Today he had rested and reflected; he had rejoiced and prayed; he knew his life would be different.

"It's time to risk," he said, trying to assure himself that it would be all right. "Tomorrow I will return to the barnyard different from the bird that left there eight days ago. Tomorrow will be more than a new day." With that, Joshua fell asleep.

CHAPTER TWELVE
T O H A V E W O R T H

The new day had barely begun when Joshua awoke full of anticipation. Today was the day he would return to the barnyard. He was excited at the thought of seeing his mother and his friends. "What will they think? So much has happened during the last week!" The sun was beginning to show in the east, bright rays silhouetting the barnyard. The buildings appeared to be on fire against the sun's backdrop.

That was Joshua's destination for today. It was time to leave the strength and security of the tree and head out. It was time to return to the old, with a new perspective. Joshua looked west at the range of mountains knowing they held his future. "No time to think of this now; I'll have plenty of time for that later."

Suddenly he felt sad. Was it the thought of leaving the tree, the thought of going back, or the unknowns of the future? It was none of these, really. It was the void he felt without Owl.

"Why did he leave? Why did he stay with me for only six days? Will I see Owl again?" he asked. Owl had been kind and sharing of both himself and his knowledge. "Maybe it was meant to be, our time together. Maybe it was time for him to leave. It's up to me now. I have to act on what I've learned."

He turned and took one last look at the mountains, as if to say, "I'll see you soon." He looked at the tree, the wonderful tree and at the birds above him. He thanked his Creator for bringing him to this place of knowledge. Looking east toward the barn, Joshua spread his wings, lifted himself to flight and began his journey back.

WHO SATISFIES YOUR DESIRES WITH GOOD
THINGS SO THAT YOUR YOUTH IS RENEWED LIKE
AN EAGLE'S. PSALMS 103:5 (NIV)

He could see them all—his mother, the other chickens, the pig, the horse and the rabbit in her cage. With each slow and powerful beat of his wings, Joshua came closer to home.

As he headed down toward the central part of the barnyard, he heard his mother rejoice, "Look everyone, it's Joshua!" The eyes of the barnyard animals turned upward as they watched Joshua's approach. He landed a few feet from his mother with the grace and precision of an eagle.

Everyone had a hundred questions and comments.

"Where have you been?"

"You can fly!"

"You look different!"

"What have you been doing?"

"Are you all right?"

"I'm glad you're back!"

Joshua patiently listened to them and answered all the questions he could. He told them how he had been drawn to the tree. He told them about meeting Owl and how the tree had become a home for him. And, most importantly, he shared with them the six elements of balance. In the dirt he scratched a picture of how one can start with Clarity and move up through Congruency, Control, Condition, Communication, ending with Closeness. He explained what each element represented and how each is an independent part of an interrelated existence.

CHAPTER THIRTEEN
T O   S E E K   B A L A N C E

"What's so important about balance, anyway?"
Joshua realized that it was a very good question. He thought for a moment about his life before and his life now. In addition, he thought about where his life could be in the future. He remembered his earlier dream, the one he'd had before he left for the eagle's tree, and how unhappy and confused he'd been.

"Before I went to the tree I was unhappy; I didn't understand why. This unhappiness was fed by wrong perceptions of reality, personal confusion, a lack of self-discipline, poor health, faulty communication and awkward relationships. I was without a sense of balance in my life.

"Balance brings perspective where fanaticism brings distortion. Far too often, I'd try for Closeness without Communication. Or, I'd try for Condition without Control. Then again, I'd try for Congruency without Clarity. I had a hundred unclear questions with no answers. Confusion created illusions and within all illusions, there is disillusionment. *Life is a journey, hard work a reality, but balance is the challenge."*

Pig, Horse and Rabbit had all been listening carefully to Joshua, along with everyone else. They again congratulated him on his newly found knowledge, as they each returned to their areas, while talking among themselves. The barnyard looked as it always had before.

The sun's mid-afternoon rays flickered across the home that Joshua had known for so long. Joshua realized how he had misled himself earlier when he tried to find the answers to his questions through comparing his life to the lives of others. "Of course Pig is happy; he knows who he is and is doing all that he was meant to do. True, Horse does indeed enjoy running free in the fields but she equally accepts the reality of the work to do and the security that barnyard life brings. So, maybe, Horse won't change things, or maybe she would if she wanted to enough. It is her choice to make. However, Rabbit would change things in a minute if she could. Now I know what she's talking about. Avoiding change for security's sake is not living life to its fullest.

Do not wear yourself out to get rich; have the wisdom to show restraint. Cast but a glance at riches, and they are gone, for they will surely sprout wings and fly off to the sky like an eagle.
PROVERBS 23:4-5 (NIV)

"The rabbit would welcome change!" Joshua proclaimed. "The lock isn't beyond my reach." So, Joshua headed toward Rabbit's cage.

At the cage, Joshua used his beak to pull at the latch until it came free.

The door swung open and Rabbit looked at the eagle and then out toward the vast openness. She was motionless as Joshua watched and waited for her to do or say something.

Finally Rabbit leaped from her cage and turned to look at Joshua. "Thank you. I don't know what's out there for me but you've given me the opportunity to explore life and find my own way."

"Always remember," Joshua told her, "that whatever life brings you, there is something within you to help you meet it. I wish you well."

As Rabbit disappeared over the horizon, Joshua wondered if they'd ever meet again and what stories they'd have to share. Watching the rabbit, Joshua felt a tug at his soul and he looked in the direction of the mountain range. The barnyard had been his home. So too, the tree had been his home. Would those mountains be his next home? Joshua now knew much more about life, but he had to act on this knowledge if he was to benefit from it.

As I watched, I heard an eagle that was flying in midair call out in a loud voice: "Woe! Woe! Woe to the inhabitants of the earth..."
REVELATIONS 8:13 (NIV)

"How easy it would be to stay here, but would it be best?" Joshua murmured. "No." Joshua realized that the answers to his questions were out there. Thanks to Owl, he at least knew the questions now: "What is my reality? What does my Creator want me to do? Which of my thoughts serves me best? What do I need to do to change? How can I take charge of my life? What must I do first? How can I improve? What skills must I learn? How can I improve my relationships?" He paused and remembered how he had always wanted to know *why*—why this?—and—why that? Joshua recalled his first meeting with Owl and how Owl had shared the importance of seeking clear questions—*seek first the clarity of your questions, then you will find your answers.* Yes, Joshua had his questions now.

It was late in the day, but he had to go and speak with his mother. He was hoping she would understand the importance of his decision.

"Joshua, do you feel you must go?" his mother asked, already knowing the answer.

"Yes, but you will never be far from me. And I will visit. You are a part of me as I am of you and that will never change," Joshua assured her. "I know more than I once knew, but less than what I will come to know. Answers I will find and as I find one answer I will most likely find several new questions. But seeking balance will be the scale that keeps me level."

"Come see us, Joshua, whenever you can," she encouraged.

"It is my own special path in life that I'm seeking. I am not leaving my life here behind; it's a part of me. The other animals here are at peace, but I have discoveries to make. It's for this reason I must go." With that, Joshua raised himself gracefully into the air and climbed upwards. Higher and higher he climbed until he was a mere soaring speck in the sky. His mother stood gazing at the sky for several minutes after the speck had disappeared. Then, she turned and began to slowly walk back to her friends.

CHAPTER FOURTEEN
E P I L O G

"**Time has passed since that day.** I have thought about Owl and Rabbit often," Joshua interjects as he stands on the rocky side of the majestic mountains, reflecting on his story. "These mountains are my home now, although I return to the barnyard and the tree whenever I feel the need. I have come to know more about balance, as you will.

"Learning is a marvelous thing. For every question you answer, you will gain a new question. Life is not, nor will it ever be, lighthearted or simple. Life has depth, width, height and balance. It is full of unexplored paths challenging your growth and maturity.

"You can choose to just live or you can choose to live because...because of visions, because of love, because of others, because of beautiful things and times and places, because of God. You exist because you were given a life; you live life to its fullest when you choose to cherish what's been given to you. So seek balance—find your own special way. Remember these things."

APPENDIX

VISIT THE WEB SITE

www.balancinglife.com

Quantity and group discounts for books and study guides are available
Fax inquiries to 1-888-726-2721 or visit the Web site

STUDY GUIDE AVAILABLE

LEARNING TO SOAR
Personal Growth & The Hierarchy of Balance

Learning to Soar STUDY GUIDE for *Joshua Worthington Eagle* helps
individuals reflect on life-changing principles. It is organized around the
Hierarchy of Intra- & Inter-Personal Balance as the psychological and
sociological backdrop. People *are* struggling with self-worth and value!
"Who am I? What is my purpose?"

Learning to Soar reflects this concern for a multitude of confused,
broken-hearted and discouraged people who question their existence. By
showing how worth, transformation and balance interrelate, they will be
drawn toward a more abundant life! *Learning to Soar,* combined with the
allegorical story *Joshua Worthington Eagle,* becomes a creative and
memorable experience in personal growth.

SEE PAGE 87 FOR MORE DETAILS ON THE STUDY GUIDE.

TO ORDER BY MAIL

If you would like to order the *Learning to Soar* STUDY GUIDE that accompanies this allegorical story, send a money order for $18.00 per copy. (Includes tax, shipping and handling)

Mail to: Balancing Life, PO Box 111557, Tacoma, WA 98411-1557

Available on disk: MS WORD .doc file **OR** ACROBAT .pdf file
PLEASE SPECIFY BELOW

ORDER FORM: (Cut or photocopy)

Print your name: _____
Address: _____
City: _____ State: _____ Zip: _____
Daytime phone:_____
I would like _____copy/ies of *Learning to Soar* supplemental material.
I have enclosed a check or money order for _____.
[ ] MS WORD .doc file   [ ] ACROBAT .pdf file
Allow 4 weeks for delivery.

Also by Samara C. Kezele Fritchman...
The Tale of Three Minds: The Chronicles of Will, Soul and Heart
Check your local bookstore or visit the Web site:
www.balancinglife.com

BOOK ORDERS

Quantity and group discounts for books and study guides are available for bulk purchases. To order this title or other materials: Fax inquiries to 1-888-726-2721 or visit the Web site.

WHY THE STUDY GUIDE?

Learning to Soar STUDY GUIDE brings to you a resource that explores the Hierarchy of Balance in a nonfiction format. *Learning to Soar* supplements *Joshua Worthington Eagle,* helping individuals reflect on life-changing principles. It is organized around the Hierarchy of Intra- & Inter-Personal Balance as the psychological and sociological backdrop. People *are* struggling with self-worth and value! "Who am I? What is my purpose?"

Learning to Soar reflects this concern for a multitude of confused, broken-hearted and discouraged people who question their existence. By showing how worth, transformation and balance interrelate, they will be drawn toward a more abundant life! *Learning to Soar,* combined with the allegorical story *Joshua Worthington Eagle,* becomes a creative and memorable experience in personal growth.

A NOTE FROM THE AUTHOR

There are theories about everything! Packaged and patterned, labeled and patterned—theories abound. I have been exposed to them; I have studied them; I have taught them; I have used them; and, I have misused them.

There are multitudes of theories for viewing people and organizations. They are useful. But they are not gospel. How often have you heard this? *"Nothing is as practical as a good theory."* However, *"Not all good theories are practical."* But, they are educational.

They provide us with a basis for formulating strategies for different situations; they enable us to memorize multitudes of information, and they lead us to develop our own theories. They make us think. Most of us can say that our experiences are full of theories gained from a combination of self-study, formal education and life experience.

However, for every neatly wrapped packaged and patterned theory, there lurks a match and an exception. So, basically, life is life. It's never as simple as these theories might suggest, nor must it be as complex.

HOW DID THE HIERARCHY COME TO BE?

As a professional educator, I'm asked by clients repeatedly to develop and present information on relationship skills. Topics, such as *Dealing with Difficult People, Communication Skills, Conflict Resolution, Leadership* and

Management Skills are popular. I realize that businesses are asking me to effect positive change in individuals through such seminars. Yet, how can a two- four- or six-hour course on *Dealing with Difficult People* produce individuals who can deal with difficult people, unless they realize their own difficult behaviors? While communication and relationship skills are the most requested courses, they are not the place to start because they deal with the higher levels of interaction—Communication and Closeness. When I began to look at training this way, I developed the *Hierarchy of Intra- & Inter-Personal Balance* and I designed seminar materials, regardless of the topic, around the hierarchy, beginning the information with Clarity, and ending with Closeness.

DEFINITIONS

Joshua Worthington Eagle explores personal growth designed around the Hierarchy of Intra- & Inter-Personal Balance. The following definitions will help clarify how the words are used.

Growth (n): A gradual increase.

Consciousness (n): Aware of one's own existence; aware of external conditions, aware of a fact.

Awareness (n): Consciousness; cognizance.

Hierarchy (n): A group of things arranged in successive order, each of which is subject to or dependent upon the others.

Intra- (prefix): Situated or occurring within.

Inter- (prefix): Situated or occurring between, or outside of.

Personal (adj.): Referring to and directly concerning an individual.

Balance (n): A state of equilibrium, harmonious proportions, as in the design or arrangements of the parts of the whole; mental and emotional stability.

Clarity (n): Clearness; lucidity, mentally sound, rational, easily understood.

Congruency (n): Harmonious; appropriate fit.

Control (v): Exercise authority over; to restrain, curb; to regulate, verify.

Condition (n): State of health; a circumstance necessary to the occurrence of some other; a prerequisite.

Communication (n): The act of imparting or transmitting ideas, information, etc., a message.

Closeness (n): Near in space/time; bound by strong affection; to come nearer together.

THE HIERARCHY OF
INTRA- & INTER-PERSONAL BALANCE

CLOSENESS
COMMUNICATION
CONDITION
CONTROL
CONGRUENCY
CLARITY

This information is a concept for living, not a concrete theory that needs to be rigidly followed. *The Hierarchy of Intra- & Inter-Personal Balance* contains six elements—*Clarity, Congruency, Control, Condition, Communication* and *Closeness.* They are interrelated, dynamic, ever-changing and continuously evolving aspects of our lives. There is no easy way to breeze through life; however, the balancing aspects of these elements provide a pattern or path. Personal balance requires as much effort as any other worthwhile pursuit.

Too often individuals try to find all their answers from the highest level, *Closeness.* Yet, how can we have nourishing relationships without clear *Communication* skills? Before positive communication skills, we must have *Condition*—looking after our mind, body and spirit. In addition, we must be able to manage ourselves—*Control*—and accept responsibility for our choices. Yet, how can we do this if we do not understand how the different parts of us—our feelings, thoughts, behavior and attitudes—*Congruently* work together. Finally, before *Congruency*, we need *Clarity*, which is the first step toward increased human potential. Clarity begins with a long, hard look in the mirror.

THINK ABOUT...

We need to be reminded more often than we need to be instructed. The real job of adult education is to keep bringing people back, time and time again, to the old, simple truths that we know.

In looking for the common thread that weaves through life, we can begin to see an on-going insistence that life and people can make sense— that all experiences provide significance!

Self-Image

We are born; then, we begin acting and reacting with our environment. Experiences, like rocks in a bucket, pile up and one side gets heavier than the other. Then, we begin to lean in that direction.

The subconscious picture we hold in our mind of ourselves controls our performance. When we leave our comfort zone our body lets us know. When we cannot get back into our comfort zone, we try to recreate our comfort zone in the new surrounding. If we do not change our internal self-image to match new surroundings, we will change the new surroundings to match our current internal self-image.

Perceptions

Individual perceptions are individual truths. A vast dichotomy exists between perceptions of reality, solutions, the right way and right answer and right belief.

We need to gain clarity about ourselves, including how we interpret the world around us, read other people, learn and process information and handle conflict.

This clarity must become an essential focus.

Attitudes

Human effectiveness has to do with attitudes. Attitudes are the direction in which we lean. They are our *habits of thought and behavior*.

Unfortunately, we are overexposed to negative experiences and interactions from a young age. These experiences and interactions create files in our mind that are full of negative attitudes.

Much of the negative feedback that we get in life comes from ourselves, from our own files. We talk to ourselves. We make many assumptions that are played out nowhere else except in our minds.

Self-Exploration

Self-exploration is to go beyond the known. It is the ability to become comfortable with the unknown—always discovering and learning.

As a unique, one-of-a-kind individual, do not look for a teacher, guru, or leader to follow in cult-like style. Instead, extract information from many sources, balancing knowledge with wisdom and faith, for the connection.

To attain emotional security we must learn to develop two critical capabilities: 1) The ability to live with uncertainties, and 2) The ability to delay gratification in favor of long-range goals.

Change

Change is the one thing in life we can count on. Insight is the initial catalyst for change. Change exposes old assumptions so we can see flawed and incorrect thinking. We may begin to understand why we do the stupid, quirky, irritating, or dogmatic things we do. We may be surprised to discover that our behavior is based on incomplete assumptions and false perceptions.

With change, emotions often rise to the surface—anger, embarrassment and uncertainty—and create a reluctance to talk about what is thought to be not discussible. This, coupled with confusion and fear, inhibits many people from completing the change process.

Choices

Remember the word *smorgasbord,* because it is a great example for learning. With a smorgasbord, there are many choices. Depending on where we are in life and the condition we are in, some of the selections are not beneficial and others are essential.

There are two primary choices in life: 1) To accept conditions as they exist, or 2) To accept the responsibilities for changing them or for viewing them differently.

Goals

Unfortunately, we are a world of impatient people. We want what we want instantaneously, even when we're not sure what we want.

Look at two prerequisites that are necessary for living a balanced life: faith and diligence. Nothing in this world can take the place of persistence. Talent will not. Genius will not.

ADDITIONAL SHORT STORIES

SOMETHING OF VALUE

The golden sun silhouetted the wooded trail with tall stately trees lining both sides of its path. The sound of birds fluttering about filled the air above. Over to the right, about twelve feet away was a cliff, which dropped off sharply to the rock-covered beach below.

The sound of water washing up to the shore below provided a soothing sensation for the moment. He was a man of great value to the Lord, the man who was walking down that wooded trail. Yet, he questioned his value, because worldly circumstances over the years had cut deeply into his heart and his soul.

As he walked, he began to cry out to his Father. Not by words, but rather by his heart; crying out for justice and understanding so as to regain the value that had been cut away from him. Each step weighed heavily and the burden of frustrating emotions soared from his soul, stinging his heart. All he seemed to be able to speak was, "Father, Father."

He stopped for a moment to look westerly over the water at the sunset. Golden and bright, the fiery sun began to drop below the distant range of mountains. It cast a shimmering light that danced across the water right toward him and he felt a peace—a moment of peace—in his tormented soul. He hung his head to pray, "Father, help me understand; where is the justice? What value am I? In return for hard work I was used; for love given, indifference was returned; for honesty expressed, lies and deceptions were received." He stood there in silence.

"Open your eyes so that I can open your heart," the Lord spoke to him. Startled by hearing the Lord's voice, he opened his eyes to see the bright reflection of the sun off a tiny, yet shiny piece of metal on the trail. It was brilliant! He reached down to pick it up. It was a coin partially covered by dirt; he freed it and drew it closer for a better look. Just as he had about wiped it clean, but before he could take a good look at it, something happened. He was looking downward at the coin in his hand when feet appeared on the ground before him. Caught by surprise he jumped backward almost dropping his recent find.

"That's something of value you have there," said an elderly man dressed in worn clothes. He had gray hair, a full head of it, with a long beard. He continued, "Didn't mean to frighten you, not at all. You've made quite a discovery there." He pointed to the golden coin in the younger man's hand.

"I haven't had a chance to look at it yet; I was just about to when you appeared," he said as he looked first at the old man and then down at the coin in his hand.

"Yes sir, son—you hold a thing of value, precious and rare," the old man spoke as they both looked at the golden coin that lay against his palm.

"I wonder where it came from?"

"From times past," the old man replied.

"How did it get here?"

"From one hand to the next."

"I wonder what it's worth?"

"It's of great value for *you*."

"For *me*?"

"Yes, for you," the old man repeated as he lifted up his hands to cradle the younger man's hands that held the coin.

"Do you know about this coin?" he asked the old man.

"Yes, I have seen others before this time."

"Tell me about it!"

"It's old, or at least as you understand time. It's from the time after Christ's death—see the angel on it holding in one hand the symbol of Christ and in the other a cross upon the world. Let's turn it over. Oh yes, an image of a man wearing armor with a crown of life on his head and a cross in his hand."

"Do you think it's made of gold? How was it made? Do you know that?"

"Yes, it's gold. A precious metal—gold. And gold becomes gold after it has stood the test of fire, burning out all impurities. For this coin to be, it had to submit to pressure to take on form. These images were struck into it when its substance was still soft and could conform to the die. One bronze die, or casting, could produce only one thousand coins before it would break under the mallet. But the die was only a temporary shell. This coin has survived, for it has stood a test of fire and pressure."

"You seem to know a lot about this coin."

"It's symbolic of you! Your flesh is the outside shell and though your flesh may break in its weakness, your heart and soul will survive because they have surely stood a test of fire and pressure. And this process in life has enabled the impurities of your life to be burned out and has provided you form.

"And, just as you hold something of great value in your hand, so too does God hold you in His hand. Just as the coin has taken on the image of Christ symbolically, so too are you conforming to His image.

"You dwell on your past so you aren't seeing your future value. You feel worn by your past. You should. This coin is worn with its usage. It has not been isolated from the world, nor should it be, for that wasn't its purpose. Nor is it yours. The coin has increased in value, just as you have. You do not seem to question the value of this coin, but you question your value. How much greater are you to the Father than this coin is to you?

"Where this coin has been is not as important as where it will go; how it's been used in the past is not as important as how it will be used in the future. So too with you, this coin by your hand and you by the Lord's.

"Close your hand around this coin—this is how the Father holds onto you. This coin was made adequate for its purpose and has lost no value over time. Would God make you any less adequate for His purpose? No, not at all! Would He allow time to rob you of your value? No, not at all!"

He stood in silence. The younger man shut his eyes and felt the coin in his palm and thanked God for having heard his prayer. He felt the hands of the old man touch his as he said, "That's something of great value you have." And in the next moment, his touch was gone.

The young man opened his eyes and found himself standing alone with a clenched fist. Had it been a dream? But as he opened his hand he saw the golden coin lying on his palm—a gift from God—bearing witness to his value.

THE MUSTARD TREE

"How quickly time has passed," she thought to herself as she sat motionless in the grassy and slightly damp yard. She reached over to the dirt in the nearby garden, sifting it through her fingers feeling its richness and life. How she loved the feel of her hands in God's Earth.

With a palm full of dirt, she sat back and let the sun's rays warm her face. Opening her eyes she looked to her right at the Mustard Tree. Actually, it was more a large shrub than a tree and she thought how weary it looked. She tossed the handful of dirt in its direction. "It is dying," she thought. But in her mind she remembered the day she planted the ever-so-small seed in the ground. It had grown with her care. She had watched it sprout through the dirt, small and fragile. She had watered it and given it stakes to lean against. She had watched it mature, becoming a resting spot for little birds. She had watched it bloom and remembered how special the petals were, shaped like a cross, each one. Then the day came when the fruit capsules split open at its maturity. Now, she was watching it die—weary from life.

"Father," she prayed, "I feel like this Mustard Tree—waning in dryness from its struggle in life." She opened her eyes and looked at it again. Crawling over toward it, she positioned herself in the dirt right next to its withering form. "Where are its seeds?" She thought as she poked about in the ground. On her hands and knees she sought a sign of but one seed. It was almost a feeling of desperation. What value has it had, if all it did was grow old only to die?

She felt a sadness prevail. Quickly she thought how much she was like this Mustard Tree—alone, her joy dimming, as weariness grew. "There must be some seeds!"

"What a marvelous plant," came the sound of a stranger's voice. Startled, the young woman jumped back falling on her bottom. Looking up she saw an elderly woman, who was taking her place next to her on the grass at the edge of the garden.

"I didn't mean to startle you, but you won't find any seeds. Were you looking for them?" inquired the older woman.

"Yes."

"What importance are these seeds to you?"

"I'm not sure, it just seems sad that this great plant is dying."

"When you planted the seed, did you think it would die?"

"No."

"Why do you think it's dying now?"

"Just look at it, drooping and weary, blooms gone, fruit capsules split open and all its seeds gone."

"Like your life?"

"Who was this woman," she thought, "and why was she here?" The elderly woman reached out her hand and laid it on her shoulder. "That's a good thing, rejoice in the likeness. You planted the seed that grew into this plant; faith and diligence blessed the work of your hand. Through Jesus a seed was planted in your heart; by faith and diligence your Father blesses you.

"You watered it when it was dry—just as the Father poured out His Spirit on you. You gave it a stake to lean on as the fullness of its life weighed heavy. So too has the Spirit held you upright. Birds made this plant a place of rest—God has made your heart a place of rest from the weariness of your soul. Many seeds burst forth from this plant, so small you cannot see those already beneath the dirt; others carried off by the birds; others by the wind. So too are the many seeds that have burst forth from your heart. Some are carried off by others; some are carried off by the Wind of the Spirit, while others stay at rest in your soul to grow bigger in due season. By God's wisdom your soul is re-seeded with holiness and joy."

"Then it's not dying?" the younger woman replied.

"Nor are you," said the elderly woman. "Life's a cycle for both this plant and for you: this plant was once a seed, like you. This plant was once young and fragile, like you. This plant was once dry and in need of life-giving water, like you. This plant was once strong and steady, like you. This plant was once in need of support, like you. This plant provided rest for the birds as you have provided rest for others. This plant was once in full bloom, like you, with such joy. This plant grew older, tired and weary, but the seeds it produced will bring forth new life for they have not fallen on barren ground, just as it is with you and your seeds.

"What you see as dying is but an outer shell. What you see as weary is just a turning point. New life, life anew, is but a season away. The Kingdom of God is like a Mustard Seed.

"The seed your faith has planted in your heart, through Jesus, tended to by the Holy Spirit and blessed by the Father has wearied with life's struggles, but new life will spring forth from its seeds.

"To think it all began with one small seed of faith in Jesus. That seed grew in your heart, large and strong, supported by the Holy Spirit. Your faith strengthened into full bloom—growing as big as the Mustard Tree—each petal a reminder of the cross; each petal blooming with joy. But for new seeds to bloom forth, the cycle must continue, and that first full bloom went dormant, not to die, but rather to be further nurtured, fed, hoed and pruned—to be reshaped by the hands of our Father in Heaven. And, with the coming new season, the life within you will once again appear. However, now it is time for you to be still. By faith you have grown and brought forth seeds of new life to be scattered into your soul—growing and spreading the Word of God—choking out the weeds the world has planted in you. It's a process, a godly cycle of life—seasons of growth and seasons of rest; seasons for you to tend; seasons for you to be tended."

The older woman sat back and looked at the blessed face of the younger woman and then they both looked at the Mustard Tree.

"Just as you have tended to and cared for this plant, so too has God tended and cared for you. If the dryness and weariness of this plant is but a rebirthing—Praise God. If the dryness and weariness of this plant is but a moment of rest—Praise God. If the dryness and weariness of this plant is but a season in life—Praise God. This plant will grow again, bloom again, seed again—Praise God. This plant by your hand and you by the Father's, for how much greater are you to Him, than this plant is to you?"

ABOUT THE AUTHOR
Samara C. Kezele Fritchman, CEAP, CMHC, NCC, JD

Samara has worked in the Employee Assistance Profession for almost twenty years with experience in business consultations, counseling, interventions and adult education. She is a public speaker with workshop leadership skills. Work projects include the development and implementation of customized training programs in business, psychology, human relations and job skills. She has worked with all levels of staff, spanning a variety of job classifications, ethnic backgrounds and educational levels. Samara is available as a presenter or workshop leader at special retreats and/or workplace conferences. She is a Certified Employee Assistance Professional through the International EAPA. She holds educational degrees in business (BA), psychology (MA) and law (JD).

NOTES